The Everlasting Christmas Tree

English text by Helen East

Original text by Renate V
Pictures by Mary F

D1638732

Macdonald

One day
in the middle of summer,
Lisa found a Christmas tree,

standing all on its own
in a clearing in the forest.
Lisa knew at once it was her special tree.

It was perfect.
Exactly the right shape
and exactly the right height for Lisa.
Just looking at it made her feel Christmassy.
She started singing Christmas carols,
and planning how to decorate it
with tinsel here, and lights there, and a fairy on top.
"But Lisa," said her mother, "it isn't your tree.
It probably belongs to the man who owns the wood."
"Did he plant it here specially?" Lisa demanded.

"Perhaps," said her father. "Or perhaps not.
Maybe the wind just blew the seed here."
"Maybe the birds brought it," said Lisa.

"So they could live in the tree.
I think it is a special bird Christmas tree,
and they want to share it with me!"

All through the autumn Lisa visited her tree.
Slowly all the other trees lost their leaves,
but the Christmas tree stayed green and bright.
Once she found a spider's web
glistening like tinsel in the branches.
A little higher up, she hung a gleaming glass ball.
It made the tree look so proud and smart.
She wished she could take it home with her
for a real Christmas,
with lights all over it, and presents piled up high.

Winter came, and at last it was almost Christmas.
Everyone was busy making things, and hiding secrets,
and decorating everywhere.
Lisa's father took out the Christmas tree baubles,
and shook last year's pine needles out of the box.
Then, suddenly, Lisa remembered.
Last year, after Christmas, when everything was over,
they had taken all the decorations off the tree.
All its pine needles had fallen off, too,
into a sad little heap on the floor.
All that was left was a bare brown stem
with spindly empty branches.

"Cheer up, Lisa!" said her mother.
"We've got a surprise," said her father.
"You can have your little Christmas tree after all.
We asked the owner, and he said yes!"
Lisa thought of her tree
and its beautiful bright green needles.
"Oh no!" she said,
and burst into tears.

The next day was Christmas Eve.
Lisa's grandparents and aunt and uncle
came to put their presents under the tree.
They looked round the house, but it wasn't there.
"Where's Lisa's tree?" they asked. "Didn't you get it?"
Lisa and her parents smiled little secret smiles.
"Come on, everyone," said Lisa. "We're going out."
"Where?" asked her aunt. "Why?" asked her uncle.
But no-one would tell them.
So they all squashed into the car
with a pile of blankets and scarves and hats,
and drove off into the mysterious darkness.

They stopped the car on the edge of the woods,
and everyone got out.
Crik! Crunch! went their boots on the frozen ground.
Under the trees was shadowy black,
but their branches were white like long snow fingers.
Lisa led the way, dancing down the path.
Her father's torch shone out, yellow and friendly.
They were almost there.
Lisa heard her mother fumbling for matches.
Her grandfather began to hum very gently.
They reached the clearing—

and there was Lisa's Christmas tree,
decorated secretly that afternoon.
"Ooh," said Lisa's granny. "Aah," said Lisa's uncle.
"Hooray!" cried Lisa, as her mother lit the candles.

They danced round the tree, admiring it all over.
Then they sang all the Christmas carols they knew.
"Look!" whispered Lisa. "You can see our songs!"
They were hanging in the air like white ice whiskers.

Carefully Lisa laid out all the presents,
some up on the branches, some under the tree.
There were nuts, fruit, seed rings,
and even a carrot.
"Come and get your presents,
birds and animals," she cried.
"Your Christmas tree is ready and waiting!"
"They won't come till we blow out
the candles, and go,"
Lisa's granny told her gently.
"But when you're tucked up in bed
they'll come hurrying out,
to have their party by the light of the stars."

Lisa's granny was right.
After Christmas, when Lisa went to see her tree,
she found hundreds of pawprints and marks all round it.
Birds, rabbits, squirrels, mice and even a deer
(Lisa thought it might have been a reindeer)
had come to the tree for their Christmas presents.
Almost everything had gone.
Something had even eaten the candles!
But the little tree still looked beautiful.
Lisa smiled as she stroked its bright green needles.
"See you next summer, Christmas tree," she promised.

A MACDONALD BOOK

© Otto Maier Verlag Ravensburg 1985
© English text Macdonald & Company (Publishers) Ltd 1987

First published in Germany in 1985
under the title of *Lisa und ihr Tannenbaum*, written by Renate Welsh.

First published in this edition in Great Britain by
Macdonald & Company (Publishers) Ltd
London & Sydney
A BPCC plc company

Printed and bound in Singapore

Macdonald & Co (Publishers) Ltd
Greater London House
Hampstead Road
London NW1 7QX

British Library Cataloguing in Publication Data
East, Helen
   The everlasting Christmas tree.
   I. Title
   823'.914 [J] PZ7

   ISBN 0-356-13755-4
   ISBN 0-356-13756-2 Pbk